Story by Alex de Campi
Art by Federica Manfredi

HAMBURG // LONDON // LOS ANGELES // TOKYO

# *Kat & Mouse Vol. 4*

Written by Alex de Campi

Illustrated by Federica Manfredi

---

Tones - Cari Stevenson
Development Editors - Carol Fox and Tim Beedle
Layout and Lettering - Michael Paolilli
Cover Designer - Chelsea Windlinger

Editor - Lillian Diaz-Przybyl
Print Production Manager - Lucas Rivera
Managing Editor - Vy Nguyen
Senior Designer - Louis Csontos
Director of Sales and Manufacturing - Allyson De Simone
Associate Publisher - Marco F. Pavia
President and C.O.O. - John Parker
C.E.O. and Chief Creative Officer - Stu Levy

A TOKYOPOP® Manga



TOKYOPOP Inc.
5900 Wilshire Blvd. Suite 2000
Los Angeles, CA 90036

E-mail: info@TOKYOPOP.com
Come visit us online at www.TOKYOPOP.com



ISBN: 978-1-4278-1175-2

First TOKYOPOP printing: September 2009

10 9 8 7 6 5 4 3 2 1

Printed in the USA

Cat & Mouse

# TABLE OF CONTENTS

PREVIOUSLY...

When her father accepts a new job teaching science at a prestigious private school in New Hampshire, Kat Foster has no choice but to pack up her things and move with her family to Dover—a wealthy community where they don't exactly fit in. Kat quickly falls to the bottom of the social ladder at her school, but she does make one new friend: Mee-Seen Huang. Mee-Seen—or "Mouse" as she prefers to be known—is a punky skateboarder who takes pride in the fact that she stands out. Kat's also made a few rivals, notably the "Chloettes," a frequently snobby trio of princesses.

Kat and Mouse have faced many challenges at Dover Academy, most of which are caused by The Artful Dodger—a mysterious thief who has been stealing valuables around campus. Kat and Mouse have vowed to bring the thief to justice. However, despite their best efforts, the identity of The Artful Dodger remains a mystery. But now Chloe's necklace has gone missing in the middle of the Dover Academy Snow Ball, and with all of her suspects conveniently in one place, it's Kat's chance to solve things once and for all!

PREVIOUSLY...
FORGET THIS STUPID DANCE. LET'S GO HOME.
WHAT ARE YOU, MOUSE? KAT'S BOYFRIEND?
BECAUSE YOU'RE DRESSED LIKE IT!
KAT, MOUSE! YOU'VE GOT TO HELP ME!
MY MOM'S DIAMOND NECKLACE—IT'S BEEN STOLEN!
JUST WHY SHOULD WE DO ANYTHING FOR YOU, CHLOE?
NO. WE ARE GOING TO HELP HER.
BECAUSE IT'S THE RIGHT THING TO DO.
BECAUSE WE AREN'T LIKE HER.
SO... DIZZY...

JUST... NEED... SOME...
FRESH... AIR...

HEY--
OOOH...
RUTH!

# Chapter 1:
# The Fallen Angel

NICK!
WHASS--
OH MY GOD.
WHAT'S WRONG WITH HER?
I DUNNO... BUT HELP ME GET HER INSIDE. SHE DOESN'T HAVE A COAT OR ANYTHING.
WOW. IT'S LIKE LIFTING A BIRD. SHE WEIGHS *NOTHING...*
HOORAY... THEY THINK I'M THIN...

THANK YOU SO MUCH.
MY PARENTS WILL KILL ME IF I DON'T GET THE NECKLACE BACK.
YEAH, UM.
WHATEVER.
HEY, CHLOE, FIRST WILL YOU PROMISE TO TELL ME THE WHOLE TRUTH ABOUT ONE THING?
CROSS MY HEART AND HOPE TO DIE!
WHO IS THE ARTFUL DODGER?

...I DON'T KNOW.
HONEST. I REALLY DON'T.
FINE.
MOUSE, LET'S SPLIT UP AND SEE IF WE CAN FIND ANYTHING IN THE GYM.
COOL! MEET BACK HERE IN TWENTY?
YEAH.
BUT CHLOE, IF YOU'RE LYING AND I FIND YOUR NECKLACE, I'M TOTALLY SELLING IT ON EBAY AND THEN MY FAMILY'S GOING TO DISNEYWORLD.
HAH!
I'M--HEH--SO NOT LYING, I PROMISE.
I WANNA GO TO DISNEYWORLD TOO!
Space Mountain RULEZ

HMMM.

HMMM....
AHA!
I KNOW WHAT'S WRONG.
EVERY GREAT DETECTIVE IS NOTHING WITHOUT HER DETECTING HAT.
AND WHAT, PRAY TELL, ARE WE DETECTING?
AAAH!

DUDE, SHE'S REALLY SHAKING.
NO... I'M FINE...
WE GOTTA FIND A TEACHER.
WE GOTTA FIND HER SOMETHING TO EAT.
MY SIS' COLLEGE ROOMMATE WAS LIKE THIS. SHE PUT ON THE FRESHMAN 15 AND TOTALLY FLIPPED.
STARVED HERSELF SO BAD SHE GOT PERMANENT HEART DAMAGE.
HER BODY, LIKE, ATE HER HEART BECAUSE IT HAD NOTHING ELSE TO EAT.
GINA WAS SEVENTEEN.
RUTH'S, LIKE, TWELVE?

MAN, WHY DO GIRLS DO THIS?
IT'S SO WACKED OUT.
SBAM
HEY.
I GOT ONE OF THOSE PROTEIN SHAKE THINGS IN MY LOCKER.
WOULD THAT HELP?
YEAH, IT MIGHT.
I'LL STAY WITH RUTH AND GRAB THE NEXT TEACHER WHO WALKS BY.
YOU GET THE DRINK.
COOL. BACK IN A FLASH.

HAS THE ARTFUL DODGER DONE SOMETHING TO GET YOU AND KAT ON THE WARPATH?
UMM...
BECAUSE THREE DETECTIVES ARE BETTER THAN TWO, YOU KNOW.
ERRRR....
OMG, YOU WOULDN'T CHLOE
"BORROWED" THIS FROM
HER MOTHER AND
I MEANT WITH AND IT GOT
STOLEN ABOUT 10 SHE IS SO
AND WE DODGER
EVEN HARSH
OF HIS BUT HE OR
WITH THAT PAINTING
AT LIKE HE'S
AND
SCHOLARSHIP KIDS
TO COME TO OF JUST
RICH FREAKS I TOTALLY HAVEN'T
DRAWN MINUTES WOW I
DO THAT.

THAT'S FANTASTIC, MOUSE.
meep!
THAT'S THE BEST NEWS I'VE HAD SINCE I ARRIVED AT DOVER ACADEMY.
Whew...
Huh...
WAIT...
BUT...
...AREN'T WE GOING TO WORK TOGETHER?

Risky. Could work.
No. The janitor might find it first.
No. The Dodger's not that obvious.
HMMM....
IF I STOLE A DIAMOND NECKLACE, WHERE WOULD I HIDE IT?
RESTR

Uh-oh... are the other school buildings open? Better check for tracks in the snow.
Ha. Awesome. No.
WARDRO

HEY.
HOW'S IT GOING?
WHERE HAVE YOU BEEN?
FIXING MY MAKEUP.
OH. IT LOOKS--
YOU LOOK NICE.
UM.
I'LL BE BACK IN A SEC. I JUST HAVE TO, UH...
...STICK MY HAND IN SOME GARBAGE.

UGH.
DROBE

ROOMS
ICK.
ICK ICK ICK.
GROSS.
UGH, WHAT **WAS** THAT?
...METAL?
SFRUSH

huff
huff
huff
SKISH
SHAAAH
HOLD ON, RUTH.
SNOW BALL 2007
huff
huff
AND NOW...

WAIT.
KIDS.
BECAUSE OF THE WORSENING WEATHER CONDITIONS...
AS WELL AS OTHER MATTERS...
WE ARE GOING TO HAVE TO LOCK THE FRONT DOORS UNTIL YOUR PARENTS BEGIN ARRIVING AT 10 P.M.
WE CAN'T RISK ANYONE...
...GETTING CAUGHT OUT IN THIS BLIZZARD.

KLACK

OH NO!

WHO--

Awww....

AAH!
KAT!

# Chapter 2: Freezeout

ARE YOU OKAY?
I'M COVERED IN SOGGY DORITOS, HALF-EATEN TWINKIES AND MOUNTAIN DEW.
I'M SO FAR FROM ALL RIGHT.
HA HA HA HA!
TWO POINTS!
BUT...
HA HA HA--
PETER PARKMAN.
I WANT A WORD WITH YOU, YOUNG MAN.
ULP!

LOOK WHAT I FOUND.
MY NECKLACE!
BUT THE DIAMONDS ARE GONE...
YOU ARE IN DEEP TROUBLE.
I DIDN'T MEAN TO PUSH HER! I JUST TRIPPED!
IT WAS AN ACCIDENT--
YOUR PARENTS CALLED. APPARENTLY YOU WERE GROUNDED?
THEY'VE HAD THE POLICE OUT LOOKING FOR YOU.

WHILE WE WAIT FOR YOUR PARENTS, WOULD YOU MIND TURNING OUT YOUR POCKETS?
AN ITEM OF VALUE HAS BEEN LOST DURING THE DANCE.
YOU TOTALLY SQUEALED!
I CAN'T BELIEVE IT! I TRUSTED YOU. NOW I'M GOING TO BE IN SO MUCH TROUBLE!
CHLOE, NO! I SWEAR WE DIDN'T TELL ANYONE!
ERM...
UM, ACTUALLY, MAYBE WE DID.

SQUEEE
SQUEEE
SKISH!

RUTH...
RUTH, WAKE UP...
NICK'S HERE. HE BROUGHT SOMETHING FOR YOU.
WHUH--
NO, IT'S OKAY. I'M FINE NOW.
GRUMBLE
OW...

HERE.
THIS STUFF IS
REALLY GOOD.
Protein
Shake
Chocolate
Flavor
NO.
TOO MANY
CALORIES.

I'M SO SORRY I'M SO SORRY I'M SO SORRY.
IF THE SCHOOL CALLS MY PARENTS ABOUT THIS I SWEAR TO GOD I WILL--
AARGH!
SHUT UP! BOTH OF YOU!
WOW, THAT ACTUALLY WORKED.
LISTEN. WE NEED TO FIND THE MISSING DIAMONDS BEFORE THEY'RE GONE FOREVER.
BUT FIRST, WE HAVE TO GET THESE TEACHERS OFF OUR BACKS.
CHLOE, MUCH AS I HATE TO SAY THIS...
...WHERE'S MIMI?
HMM... I DUNNO.

I THINK SHE WENT HOME. I'LL TEXT HER...
PERFECT!
CHLOE, YOU AND MOUSE GO TELL MR. TEMPLAR THERE'S BEEN A MISTAKE.
SAY MIMI CALLED FROM HOME AND SHE'S GOT THE NECKLACE.
WHY WOULD MIMI HAVE IT?
WHY DO WE HAVE TO GO TELL MR TEMPLAR?
I DON'T KNOW. MAYBE SHE ACCIDENTALLY GRABBED YOUR BAG INSTEAD OF HERS. MAKE SOMETHING UP.
AND MOUSE, YOU BROKE IT, YOU FIX IT.
BUT YOU *LOVE* FIXING THINGS! WHY DON'T YOU FIX IT?
BECAUSE I'VE GOT DIAMONDS TO FIND.

OKAY, RUTH, LET ME GIVE IT TO YOU STRAIGHT.
YOU.
LOOK.
AWFUL!
NO, LET ME FINISH.
AND THAT'S A TRAGEDY, BECAUSE OUT OF ALL THE CHLOETTES--
MIMI THE DWARF TWIGLET--
AND CHLOE, WHO WEARS MORE MAKEUP THAN A TELEVANGELIST'S WIFE--
DUDE...
HEY, WATCH IT!
...YOU WERE THE BEAUTIFUL ONE.

I HAVE A REALLY BIG BUTT.
SAYS WHO?
FASHION MAGAZINES?
UM... CLOTHES SIZES?
AND COMPARED TO ACTRESSES ON TV?
STUPID.
WOMENS.
GARBAGE.
HAVE YOU EVER ASKED A GUY ABOUT THE RELATIVE SIZE OF YOUR REAR?
NO, YOU CLEARLY HAVE NOT.
BELIEVE ME, FASHION MAGAZINES, CLOTHES DESIGNERS AND ACTRESSES ON TV DO NOT SPEND NEARLY AS MUCH TIME STARING AT BUTTS AS YOUR AVERAGE TEENAGE GUY.
I NOW TURN YOU OVER TO MY COLLEAGUE, DR. NICHOLAS TARKINGTON III, PROFESSOR OF BUTT-OLOGY.

DR. TARKINGTON, INQUIRING MINDS WANT TO KNOW. WHAT DO *YOU* PREFER IN A BUTT?
WELL, MR. KIM, I'M AN ADVOCATE OF WHAT'S CALLED THE "APPLE" SHAPE, WHICH CONSISTS OF A NICE FULLNESS AND WIDTH ON TOP, A PLEASANT AMOUNT OF MOVEMENT WHEN WALKING, AND A GOOD FIRM SHAPE UNDERNEATH.
AS EPITOMISED BY MISS RUTH HERE, BEFORE HER UNFORTUNATE BRAINWASHING BY THE SKINNY BRIGADE.
DR. TARKINGTON, SINCE YOU MENTION IT, WHAT IS YOUR VIEW ON SKINNY GIRLS' BUTTS?
NO TUSHIE, NO NOOKIE.
SEE? THERE YOU GO. TWO OUT OF TWO EXPERTS AGREE.
SO PLEASE. EAT SOMETHING.
BE NORMAL.
BE NATURAL.
DON'T BECOME ONE OF THOSE DESPERATE NEUROTIC CHICKS, CONCERNED ABOUT EVERY POUND.
THEY'RE *REALLY* UGLY.

JUST BE YOUR BEAUTIFUL SELF, THE WAY GOD INTENDED YOU TO BE.

# Chapter 3:
# Vicious Interlude

MY FRIEND WENT OUTSIDE! WHY CAN'T I GO OUT?
NICE TRY. NOBODY'S BEEN OUTSIDE.
BUT LOOK!
HEY! WHAT ARE YOU DOING?
SOMEONE HAS BEEN OUTSIDE.
THIS IS AN EMERGENCY. THOSE ARE MY FRIEND'S FOOTPRINTS.
I HAVE TO GO OUT AND FIND HIM.
UM, OR HER.
I'M SORRY.
GO TELL THE PRINCIPAL-- SHE CAN SEND SOMEONE AFTER YOUR FRIEND.
AARGH!

WARDROB
STOMP
STOMP
STOMP
STOMP
STOMP
STOMP
STOMP
SQUIS
"SQUISH"?

WARDR
OH!

THERE THEY ARE!

........
HEY, MR. TEMPLAR! GUESS WHAT?
PETER'S MOTHER IS FURIOUS SHE CAN'T COME AND GET HIM RIGHT AWAY.
AND I'M HAVING OTHER PARENTS CALL UP WHO WANT TO PICK UP THEIR KIDS BEFORE THIS BLIZZARD GETS WORSE.
STEPHEN, I JUST CAN'T--
NOW GERALDINE, YOU KNEW YOU MIGHT HAVE TO DIVERT FROM SCHOOL POLICY...
...WHEN YOU CALLED IN THE FBI TO THE SCHOOL.
!!!

I JUST WANTED YOU TO REASSURE PRINCESS MARIE-LOUISE'S SECURITY ADVISERS...
IN OTHER WORDS, YOU DIDN'T ACTUALLY WANT ME TO *DO* ANYTHING.
I'M SORRY, GERALDINE, THAT'S NOT THE WAY THE FBI WORKS.
THIS THIEF OF YOURS IS A SERIOUS THREAT, AND I'M GOING TO END IT. TONIGHT.
OH.
MY.
GOD.

ARDROB
KAAAT!!!!
HE'S WHAT?!
THIS IS NOT GOOD.
I CAN'T BELIEVE I HAD A CRUSH ON HIM.
THE THIEF MUST BE MIMI! SHE'S THE ONLY ONE MISSING! I CAN'T BELIEVE SHE'D STEAL MY NECKLACE...
That total cow!
IT'S NOT MIMI.
I THINK I KNOW WHO IT IS.
AND WE HAVE TO WARN THEM.

I NEED TO BORROW YOUR PHONE.
OKAY.
NO!
CHLOE, DON'T GIVE HER YOUR PHONE!
SHE'LL WRECK IT TO MAKE SCIENCE STUFF!
I JUST WANT TO SEND AN SMS.
Overreact, much?
OKAY. MOUSE, GRAB YOUR COAT. WE'RE SNEAKING OUT.
Tp
Tp
CHLOE, I NEED YOU TO CLEAN UP THE NECKLACE SETTING AND SEE IF YOU CAN BEND IT BACK--
--HEY!

SORRY.
THAT'S OKAY. COME ON, MOUSE, YOU'LL NEED YOUR COAT.
WHERE ARE WE GOING?
WHEREVER THOSE FOOTPRINTS LEAD.
AND YOU'RE SURE THIS HAS NOTHING TO DO WITH MIMI?
OOOF!
YUP.
I'VE ALWAYS KNOWN IT WASN'T MIMI. EVER SINCE SHE AND PETER TRIED TO BLACKMAIL MY DAD.
YEAH. MIMI'S TOO STUPID TO BE THE ARTFUL DODGER.
And ugly. Did I mention ugly?

I GUESS.
THANK YOU. AND...
...GOOD LUCK.
NOT IF I CAN HELP IT.

IF U DO THIS 4 ME I WILL GO OUT W U
SO I'M STUPID, HUH?
FINE.
YOU RUIN MY NIGHT, MOUSE...
...I'LL RUIN YOURS.

BEEP
BEEP
BEEP
BEEP
MY PHONE!

EW.
I MEAN, SERIOUSLY.
EW.
BUT...
...UNDER ALL THAT EW...
...THE SETTING HASN'T BEEN BROKEN OR ANYTHING.
FSSSHH
I NEED A WORD WITH YOU.
CHLOE.

AAH!
SURE. BUT CAN YOU GIVE ME A MINUTE?
I'VE GOT REALLY BAD GIRL PROBLEMS.
UH...
AND I NEED TO GET A YOU KNOW WHAT FROM MY BAG.
THANKS! I KNEW YOU'D UNDERSTAND!
Sucker...
WARD
WOO!
SECRET AGENT CHLOE, FOXIN' THE FBI.

PAF
SO?
SO WHAT?
SO WHO IS IT?
THE ARTFUL DODGER?
SOMEBODY WITH ABSOLUTELY NO MOTIVE WHATSOEVER.
You could even say an anti-motive.
WHICH IS REALLY CONFUSING.
ALSO, I THINK WE'VE RUN OUT OF FOOTPRINTS TO FOLLOW.

RATS.

HMMM.
I THOUGHT YOU KNOW WHO THE ARTFUL DODGER IS.
SO?
SO YOU KNOW WHERE HE'D GO.
Kids at Dover only hang out where their clique hangs out.
WELL...
YIKES!
Snowball? What snowball?
!!

MOUSE, YOU'RE A GENIUS!
TO THE BOY'S LOCKER ROOM, GIRL WONDER!
DER NER NER NER NER NER...
NUH NUH NUH NUH NUH NUH...
NUH-NUH!

HOLY GUACAMOLE, BAT-KAT!
FOOTPRINTS!
IT'S MORE SHELTERED HERE. NEW SNOW HASN'T COVERED THE STEPS YET.
WHOA, IT'S REALLY ICY!
BE CAREFUL!
THOSE STAIRS WOULD BE NO FUN AT ALL TO FALL DOWN.
NO.
NO THEY WOULDN'T.

GOT A MESSAGE FROM MIMI FOR YOU, FREAK.
PLEASE TELL ME IT'S NOT "HAVE A NICE TRIP."
ER...
WHATEVER.
NO!

PETER, STOP!

"YOU CAN'T LET BAD THINGS HAPPEN AND JUST TURN YOUR HEAD LIKE IT HAS NOTHING TO DO WITH YOU."

"I'M SORRY. YOU DON'T KNOW HOW HARD IT IS--"

NO--
I DIDN'T MEAN TO--
CHLOE, WAKE UP...
PLEASE WAKE UP...

PLEASE...
UNGGGH...
CHLOE, I'M SO SORRY!
ARE YOU OKAY?
I DIDN'T MEAN TO HURT YOU, HONEST!

# Chapter 4:
# The Artful Dodger

I SUGGEST YOU LEAVE NOW.
BEFORE I SHOW YOU WHAT HURT FEELS LIKE.
PLEASE DON'T TELL ON ME.
GO.
SNIFF...

KAT!
KAAAAT!!
I'M FINE.
GIVE ME A HAND MOVING CHLOE INSIDE?
SHE'S HEAVIER THAN SHE LOOKS.

THERE.
WELL?
WHICH ONE?

PLEASE.
DON'T.
YOU'RE DESTROYING MORE THAN YOU COULD EVER KNOW.
YOU'VE ALREADY DESTROYED A FAIR AMOUNT YOURSELF.
MOUSE, CAN YOU...?
NERD, PLEASE.
BAM
Ka-chink

ERM...
KAT...
WERE WE SUPPOSED TO FIND SOMETHING IN THERE?

HEY, THAT'S NICK'S LOCKER!
WHAT ARE YOU GUYS DOING IN THERE?
I THINK, UM...
...KAT EXPECTED TO FIND YOUR DIAMONDS IN THERE.
ARE YOU CRAZY?
NICK'S MY BOYFRIEND. NO WAY HE'D STEAL MY NECKLACE!
Z'DANE
YOU KNOW, MY MOM HAS ALWAYS WANTED A DIAMOND NECKLACE.
SHE LOOKS LONGINGLY AT TIFFANY ADS IN MAGAZINES.

SHE KNOWS WE COULD NEVER AFFORD ONE.
SO SHE TRIES TO DO THIS WHEN NOBODY'S WATCHING.
BUT OCCASIONALLY MY DAD WILL CATCH HER.
A COPY OF VOGUE STUCK UNDER A COOKBOOK...
AND BECAUSE HE'S EMBARRASSED...
...HE'LL CHANGE THE SUBJECT TO SCIENCE, BECAUSE THAT'S WHAT HE'S COMFORTABLE WITH.
AND HE'LL SAY...
ZIDAN
"BET YOU DIDN'T KNOW DIAMONDS ARE INVISIBLE IN A GLASS OF WATER."

YOU ARE OUT OF YOUR MIND.
You and your entire family.
QUITE POSSIBLY.
WE'LL KNOW FOR SURE IN ABOUT TWO SECONDS.
MOUSE?
POUR AWAY, CRAZY PERSON.

LOOK... MY HANDS ARE FULL OF STARS!

BUT NICK...
THE ONE THING I STILL DON'T UNDERSTAND IS...
...WHY?!
I...
I TRIED TO TELL YOU.
"CHLOE?"
I CLIMBED ONTO YOUR BALCONY THE DAY AFTER THE GAME.

BUT IT WASN'T YOU I FOUND THERE.
IT ALL STARTED OFF AS A JOKE.
A WAY NOT TO BE THE MODEL STUDENT.
HAVE SOME FUN.
MOCK HOW POMPOUS DOVER ACADEMY IS.
BUT THEN...
THEN I DECIDED...
reserved

... TO DIVORCE MY PARENTS.
I NEEDED MONEY FOR THE LAWYERS. NOT MY PARENTS' MONEY.
AND I FIGURED AFTER THIS I'D BE GOING TO PUBLIC SCHOOL, SO YOU'D PROBABLY NEVER SPEAK TO ME AGAIN ANYWAY.
MAY I?

HERE.
I'LL BE GROUNDED FOR, LIKE, THE NEXT MILLION YEARS...
...BUT THERE ARE MORE IMPORTANT THINGS IN LIFE THAN SPARKLY ROCKS.
I'LL ALWAYS TALK TO YOU, DOOFUS.
EVEN IF YOU GO TO PUBLIC SCHOOL.
BLECH!

BAAAARF.
ACK.
PUKE!
VOM.
OKAY, MOUSE, YOU MADE YOUR POINT.
YIKES!

FBI AGENT, 12 O'CLOCK!
WHAT?!
MR. TEMPLAR'S FBI. SENT HERE TO CATCH YOU AS APPARENTLY YOU'RE A SECURITY RISK FOR PRINCESS MARIE-LOUISE.
WE TOTALLY GUESSED THAT, BECAUSE HE WASN'T ON GOOGLE ANYWHERE.
EXCEPT WE DIDN'T, BECAUSE WE WERE TOO BLINDED BY LUUURVE.
DIE.
STILL...
WHAT ARE WE GOING TO DO?
RUN.

RUN WHERE?
THIS THING HAS TO END FOR GOOD TONIGHT.
AND WE SHOULD BE THE ONES TO END IT.
OUR WAY.
YEAH. THIS IS OUR BUSINESS.
THE ADULTS WILL JUST MESS THINGS UP.
WORD. LET'S DO IT.

WHY DO I HAVE TO DO IT?
YOU BROKE IT, YOU FIX IT!
HURRY!
OH.
HI, MR. TEMPLAR! I WASN'T FEELING WELL...
WE WENT FOR A WALK.
These are not the droids you are looking for.
IT'S SO PRETTY WHEN IT'S SNOWING!
DOVER ACADEMY
DA

MOUSE SAID YOU LOST THAT...
IT WAS IN MY COAT POCKET.
Silly me!
I MIGHT HAVE EXAGGERATED.
THE TWINKIES TOLD ME TO DO IT.
Too much high-fructose corn syrup makes me hear voices.
DOVER
NOBODY WAS SUPPOSED TO LEAVE THE AUDITORIUM.
SORRY.
OH, AND KAT?
YOUR MOM'S HERE TO PICK YOU UP.

GAAAH!
IS IT 10:15 ALREADY?
SORRY GUYS, WE GOTTA GO!
Hell hath no fury like a mother forced to wait in the car.
HEY, CAN I GRAB A RIDE HOME WITH YOU?
ME TOO!
You go right by my place anyway.
I'LL CHECK WITH MY MOM BUT IT SHOULD BE OKAY
C'MON!
I CALL SHOTGUN!

RUSTLE
SIGH.
WHA--?

IF YOU WON'T TELL
WE WON'T TELL ON YOU
LOVE
THE ARTFUL DODGER
(WHO HEREBY ANNOUNCES HIS RETIREMENT)
AND FRIENDS

SCRUNCH

AGENT UTAH, REPORTING.
YEAH, I'M DONE HERE. REQUESTING REASSIGNMENT.

BAD NEWS, UTAH. THE ONLY OPEN ASSIGNMENT NOW IS THE XXXXXX* OP.
YOU REMEMBER, THE PEOPLE WHO TRIED TO XXXXX* THE PRESIDENT WITH A XXXXX IN XXXXX*?
YEAH, I REMEMBER.
IT'S A SUICIDE MISSION, UTAH.
I'LL TAKE IT.
FANATICAL TERRORISTS WILL SEEM LIKE A WALK IN THE PARK, AFTER THE KIDS OF...
DOVER ACADEMY
* censored by the Department of Homeland Security

WHO'S FOR HOT CHOCOLATE?
ME!
THE END

# Bonus Art from Kat & Mouse!

THANKS FOR READING!
~THE KAT & MOUSE TEAM

SEE YOU LATER!

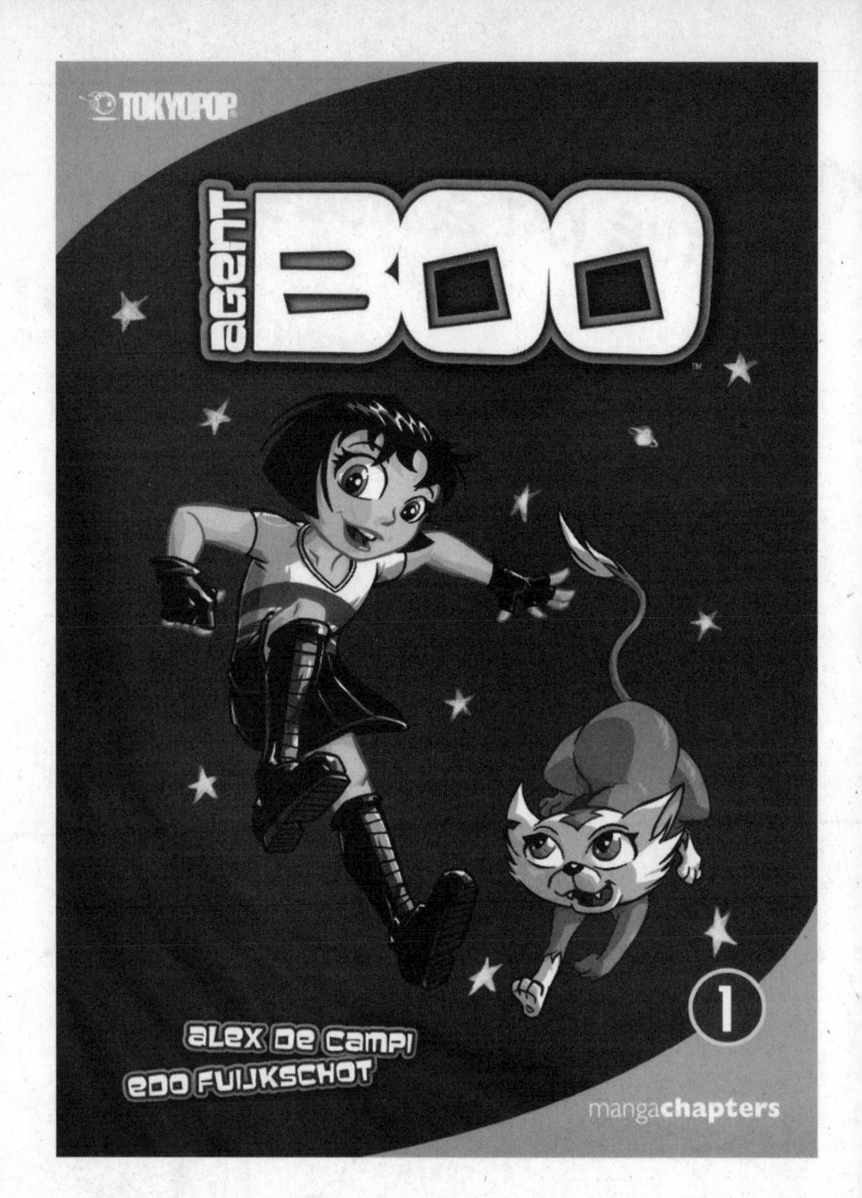


**Read on for a taste of another exciting title by writer Alex de Campi!**

## CHAPTER 1

## Singled Out in Space City

Boo slumped in her seat as the senior class walked into the auditorium and toward the stage. They passed by the fourth grade section, but they might as well have been in one of the Parallel Worlds. There was Lize, singing the school anthem in her high, perfect voice. There was Kira, blonde and confident, the smartest girl in school. There was Marcus, who already had his space-pilot's license. And there was Asano, the school's best slam-ball player until he got thrown off the team.

Asano looked up at Boo's class and smiled as if to say, "Ha ha, you still have eight more years of school."

Asano winked at some of the taller girls in Boo's class. The girls giggled and waved.

But Asano hadn't even seen Boo, because she was so small. For the five hundredth time, Boo wished that she would grow. That one morning she'd wake up tall and pretty like Kira, or super-talented like Asano. Anyone but the littlest, most picked-on girl in the fourth grade.

Then an electric silence filled the huge auditorium.

A thousand students leaned forward in their

seats, and a hundred seniors stood straighter on the stage.

At last, the Agents were making their entrance.

The Agents! Boo stretched herself as tall as she could to look. The Agents built this city—Space City, the very center of the Multiverse. From the Aerie, Space City's highest tower, the Agents kept law and order across a thousand parallel worlds.

The Agents! Every kid in Space City grew up on stories of their adventures. The Arachnoverse War . . . The Madrassa Incident . . . Agent Erik's heroic sacrifice . . . Misery's Exile . . .

The Agents! Their job was so dangerous that each autumn they would pick new trainees from the senior class to replace the Agents who had fallen in the course of duty. That's what they were doing now.

The Supreme Agent stepped forward.

"We have three vacancies at the Aerie." Her voice rang out across the auditorium, calm and proud. "As is tradition, each fallen Agent's companion will today select a new master."

"Quoth, do you see a student you would choose as Master, and advise in the ways of being an Agent?" the Supreme Agent said to a bright-eyed raven.

The raven shook his wings, flew up in the air, and looked down on the senior class. Marcus bit his lip nervously. Kira stepped closer to him and took his hand.

Asano rolled his eyes and made a loud kissing sound.

Kira glared at Asano. "Bring it," Asano hissed back.

"Though he is to Erik as day is to night,
My choice could be no other.
So it is with pride and great delight
I select my late Master's brother,"

recited the raven, landing on the shoulder of . . .

. . . Asano! "Well, that figures," said one of the girls sitting near Boo. "I mean, his brother DID save the Multiverse."

Asano reached up, dizzy with wonder, to scratch the feathers of his new friend and partner. "Join us, Agent Asano," said the Supreme Agent, holding out her hand.

Proudly, Asano walked over to where the Agents stood, not forgetting to stick his tongue out at Kira as he walked by. Aghast, Quoth the raven whispered to Kira, "Apologies, Miss; he's new at this."

"That's okay," said Kira to the raven. "Good luck."

Next came a small badger.

“Seeker, do you see a student you would choose as Master, and advise in the ways of being an Agent?”

The badger chewed his paw and glanced at the seniors. His voice was thin and faint.

“I’m just a wee, timorous beastie, an’ adventures give me a panic! I need a Master courageous and true. So I pick . . .”

A thousand students held their breath as the shy little badger waddled toward the ninety-nine seniors and reached out a quaking paw to . . .

. . . Kira! Kira swept Seeker up in her arms and smoothed all his fur. Immediately, Seeker stopped shaking.

"Join us, Agent Kira," said the Agent Leader.

As Kira left the seniors, she winked at Marcus and whispered, "See you soon."

Now from the Agents strode a big ginger cat, twitching his tail in a rocksteady beat as his eyes swept the auditorium like green searchlights.

"Pumpkin, do you see a student—"

"Yeah, yeah, yeah, Master, advise, Agent," the cat interrupted. "Lemme have a look-see at what we got." And with that, he strutted up to the seniors.

Lize flicked her hair and sang a few perfect notes. But Pumpkin just sighed and walked on. An athlete named Will grinned and flexed his perfect muscles. But Pumpkin shook his head and walked on. Then came Marcus, who turned his shoulder to show Pumpkin the badge he'd earned for his perfect score on the space-pilot's exam . . .

MAYBE THE THIRD ONE'S THE CHARM.
OH, BROTHER.
LOOK, I CAN'T DO THIS ANYMORE.

I'M TIRED.
I'M BORED.
I NEED A VACATION.
AND NONE OF THESE KIDS HAVE EVER HAD AN ORIGINAL THOUGHT IN THEIR LIVES.
I'M OUTTA HERE.
PUMPKIN! YE CANNAE DO THAT!
OH, YEAH?
EXIT
WELL, TALK TO THE TAIL, 'CUZ THE FACE AIN'T INTERESTED.
SEEKER'S RIGHT, PUMPKIN. IF YOU DON'T CHOOSE A NEW MASTER...
...YOU KNOW WHAT WILL HAPPEN.
gulp!

ALL RIGHT.
FINE.
WHATEVER.
I CHOOSE...
YOU!

"Hey! That's not fair!" yelled one of the seniors on the stage.

"Yeah, well, for those of you not keeping score, LIFE'S NOT FAIR," Pumpkin roared.

"Pumpkin . . . are you SURE of your choice?" asked the Supreme Agent.

Her second-in-command, Agent Abbot, hurriedly consulted a notebook. "There's no rule against it," he whispered.

The Supreme Agent sighed and extended her hand. "Nothing we can do, then. Very well. Join us, Agent . . . er . . ."

"Boo," squeaked Boo.

". . . Agent *Boo*."